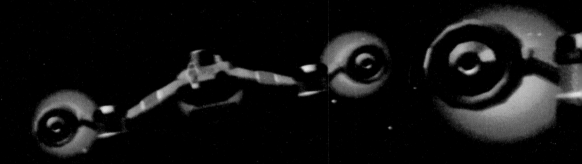

The Last Starfighter™ Storybook adapted by Lynn Haney from the novel by Alan Dean Foster • based on a screenplay by Jonathan Betuel • Copyright © 1984 by MCA Publishing, a Division of MCA, Inc. • All rights reserved • *The Last Starfighter* is a trademark of Universal/Lorimar joint venture and licensed by Merchandising Corporation of America, Inc. and Lorimar Licensing Co. • Published in the United States of America by G.P. Putnam's Sons. Published simultaneously in Canada by General Publishing Co. Limited, Toronto. • Library of Congress Cataloging in Publication Data: Haney, Lynn. The last starfighter storybook. Summary: After breaking a record by scoring over one million on the Starfighters video game, Alex is recruited by beings from the planet Rylos to fight in a war to save the universe. [1. Science fiction. 2. Video games—Fiction] I. Foster, Alan Dean, date. Last starfighter. II. Title.PZ7.H1935Las 1984 [Fic] 84-4924 ISBN 0-399-21078-4 • Printed in the United States of America Book design by Irmgard Lochner.

First Impression

THE LAST STARFIGHTER

STORYBOOK

ADAPTED BY LYNN HANEY

FROM THE NOVEL BY ALAN DEAN FOSTER
BASED ON A SCREENPLAY BY JONATHAN BETUEL

G.P. Putnam's Sons, New York

GREETINGS, STARFIGHTER! YOU HAVE BEEN RE-CRUITED BY THE LEAGUE TO DEFEND THE FRON-TIER AGAINST XUR AND THE KO-DAN ARMADA!

The strong voice from the video game cut through the stagnant California air, demanding and full of cosmic import.

Alex Rogan let his fingers dance easily over the controls on the new game, which stood proudly on the wooden porch of the general store next to the Starlite Starbrite trailer park.

The small village, in the midst of low scrub hills, consisted of perhaps a dozen vintage trailers. And the rickety general store was the center of the contented community's social life.

The videoscreen was alive with flashing, rapidly changing lights. These images fascinated Alex's ten-year-old brother Louis who stood next to him watching and trying to learn.

Alex was a master at video games. But this Starfighter was much more complex than most, with half again as many controls to manipulate. On the screen the command ship appeared. It loomed large on the simulated battle screen.

"APPROACHING KO-DAN COMMAND CRAFT," the game announced formally. "PREPARE FOR FINAL CON-FRONTATION." Miniature glowing ships suddenly proliferated on the screen. "ENEMY SQUADRONS IN SECTORS THREE, SIX, SEVEN; CLOSING FAST."

Alex turned and saw his girlfriend Maggie exiting from the side gate of her yard carrying a picnic basket, towels and a small ice chest. At the same time a bright red Dodge pickup filled with kids in bathing trunks and bikinis rolled into the parking lot in front of the store. Jack Blake, a rich and mean redneck who owned the pickup, was behind the wheel, racing the oversize engine.

"Silver Lake! The picnic. I forgot!" Alex started to run after Maggie when he heard a voice he could not easily dismiss.

"Alex?"

Wincing, he turned to look back toward his trailer. It was his mom, sure enough, leaning out one window.

"Alex, Elvira's electric is out again."

"Ah, Mom. That'll take all day."

Jane Rogan nodded, looked sympathetic, but she needed Alex. "I'm working lunch and dinner at the café. I'll be gone until tonight."

Alex sighed, knowing that he'd already lost the battle. Turning back to the truck, he sought Maggie's eyes. Somehow she managed to look twice as pretty as any other girl in town even in her baggy old sweatshirt. "You better go ahead, Maggie. I'll see you around here this evening."

Maggie understood; he could tell by the look on her face as the pickup pulled out, but it was little consolation.

At the end of the day, Alex returned to the porch to bury his sorrows and frustrations in the Starfighter game. As he worked the controls he thought about the picnic he'd missed because his mother, Jane Rogan, manager of the trailer park, had deputized him to be her repairman. What worried Alex was that one day he not only might be handling the repairs but might be taking over the operation of the whole business, as well. Now there was a safe, secure, lethally dull path, Alex thought, one that if he ever fell into, he would never escape.

The machine exploded with whizzes and explosions and mock commands and Alex was drawn back into the game. He

methodically worked his way into the rarified strata beyond half a million points.

"Yeah, yeah," he muttered aloud, impatient as always with the basics.

"PREPARE FOR TARGET LIGHT PRACTICE, STARFIGHTER," the machine warned in the same tone as always.

"Ready," Alex murmured, as if the machine could hear and understand.

Maggie, back from the picnic, climbed the steps onto the porch and rose on her tiptoes to give Alex a peck on the cheek. At the same time, the game let loose with a flurry of bright lights and electronic sound effects. Alex had advanced to still another level.

Maggie took a minute to study the videoscreen. "Hey, nine hundred twenty thousand. I thought you told me this machine can't score over a million."

"I don't see how it can," Alex replied, concentrating on his work. "It isn't calibrated past nine ninety nine."

"PACKS LOW . . . LIFE SUPPORT PLUS TWO AND FUNCTIONING . . . PHOTONIC LOW . . ." The machine delivered its announcements in clipped, precise artificial tones, indifferent to everything else.

"You're going to bust it, Alex," said Otis Davis, an old trailer park dweller who had joined them on the porch. "Hey, everybody. Listen up! Alex is going for the record. He's going to bust the machine!"

"You can't bust these machines, Otis."

"Then what happens if you hit a million?"

"I don't know . . . but it won't bust. Will it?"

A couple of regulars who'd been sitting outside soaking up the evening cool had heard Otis's exclamation and, attracted by the thought of one of their own doing something a little out of the ordinary, strolled over to see what was going on. They were nearly knocked down as other residents of the trailer park pushed and shoved past them to get the best vantage point around the machine. Alex's brother, Louis, was in the lead and edged his way up close.

"Wow, you never got this far before, Alex!" Louis was so excited that he kept bouncing up and down in front of the machine and Alex had to nudge him aside with an elbow. "Look out!" Louis yelled "Get 'em, Alex. Get 'em!"

"ENERGY WEAPONRY ON RESERVE . . . LIFE SUPPORT CRITICAL . . . PHOTONICS AT PEAK . . ." the machine declared.

In the split second available for making a decision, Alex boosted speed toward his attacker. The photonics exploded harmlessly. Before a second wave could be fired in defense, Alex's fingers stabbed on the fire control buttons, and the image of the alien command ship exploded! The subsequent bright flare of light shrank pupils all around the screen, making some of the onlookers wince involuntarily. The score limned by the red LED readout above the action rolled over past nine hundred ninety-nine thousand while the synthesized voice inside the console screamed triumphantly, "REC-ORD BREAKER, RECORD BREAKER!"

The lights faded. The screen blanked, then lit again briefly with the words, "CONGRATULATIONS STARFIGHTER."

"Wow." Louis's voice was reverent. "You really blew it away, Alex. What happens now?"

Trying to sound nonchalant, Alex gave a little shrug and turned diffidently away from the console. "Got to find a tougher game, I guess. No point in playing this one anymore." But Alex was pleased.

Alex swung a protective arm around Maggie and walked her home. Later they snuggled close on the worn porch swing in Alex's front yard, luxuriating in the cool evening air.

Maggie's face turned upward toward Alex, and their eyes locked. Alex bent forward, lips straining for Maggie's . . . but Maggie dodged neatly, kissing him on the cheek. Then she rose from the swing and headed for her front door.

"Night, Alex."

"'Night, Alex'? What's 'night, Alex'? Hey, wait." He caught up to her as she started up the steps. "What's wrong?"

Maggie hesitated at her door. "I guess it finally hit me, Alex. You're going away from here, aren't you?"

"Of course I'm going away. Do you think I want to spend my life checking plumbing and plunging toilets? We're both going away."

"Both of us?" Maggie frowned.

"Yeah, both of us. I'll go to college, find a place, get a job and come back for you."

"I didn't think you were serious about that, Alex. I thought you were just talking through your hat."

"Naw. I always talk through my lips. See?" He stuck out his chin and pointed to his puckered lips. "I . . . am . . . coming . . . back for you . . . Got it?" He smiled.

"Oh, Alex, I love you so much." Maggie put her arm around Alex and hugged him tight.

"This came for you, Alex. I was so excited, I opened it. It's about your loan . . ." Alex's mother handed him a letter.

Jane Rogan looked uncomfortable and sad. "They say you don't have enough collateral and your SAT scores aren't high enough . . . I know how much it meant to you, Alex, but you can still go to City College with your friends."

Alex felt queasy, as if he'd just eaten something he shouldn't have. He turned and fled from the trailer and ran up the driveway to the highway. In the wash of the sputtering Starlite Starbrite sign, he reread the rejection letter, finally letting it slip through his fingers to the ground. It didn't matter. Just like Mom said, he could go to City College. But he didn't want to go to City College. He wanted to go to the university. He wanted out—out of the county, out of the state, out of the Starlite Starbrite and all it stood for.

BLEEP! POP! BUZZ! BLIP! Behind Alex the video game was lighting up in a way it never had before, pulsing colors, casting an eerie glow against the porch roof. Alex went into the general store to check on what was wrong when a dark shape suddenly loomed on the road, just inside the glow of the store's lights. It was large and boxy and unusually long. Some kind of customized van. With a faint mechanical whirring, a gull-wing door opened and a voice called out, "Hello? Excuse me, son?"

Alex walked toward the car, trying to get a good look at the interior without seeming to stare. "That's a neat car, mister."

"Thanks. I try to keep it in shape."

"Foreign job?"

"It's an import, yes."

Something inside the car moved, and Alex saw a dimly illuminated face. It was an elderly face, male, lined but without the deep creases of true old age. When the driver looked up, Alex was startled by the clarity of his eyes. They might have been transparent protective lenses shielding some deeper secret from sight.

"I am here looking for someone," said the man, lighting his cigarette in a golden holder. "Can you tell me the name of the person who broke the record on that game over there?"

Pride overwhelmed Alex's caution. "His name's Alex Rogan, mister, and you're looking at him. Who're you?"

"Centauri's the name. I invented Starfighters. We must talk on a matter of utmost importance. Step into my office."

Alex started around the hood, then hesitated on reaching the other side of the vehicle. The old man looked straight, and he seemed honest. Maybe he worked for the company that made the Starfighter game. Maybe there was some kind of electronic relay built into the console that sent the results back to headquarters. Maybe he was here to give him a prize. Still, there was the fancy car, and the fact that it was dark and quiet out. Alex read the papers. He didn't want to end up a surprised corpse in some irrigation ditch. He had an idea.

"You say you invented Starfighter? Then tell me what appears on the screen on the eighth-level attack?"

Centauri didn't hesitate. "Ko-Dan Pack Fighters in squads of six guarding six landing ships equipped for taking control of civilian targets."

Alex relaxed and climbed into the cabin. No passing weirdo would know that.

The interior of Centauri's car was more spacious than he'd expected. There was lots of legroom and a complex array of digital instrumentation visible all around, none of which he recognized. The back of the car was solid. There was no rear window.

"Did I win something for my score? Is that why you're here?" Alex asked.

"What, win something? You might say that. Your achievement has entitled you to receive a great honor."

Visions of enough money to pay his way through the university immediately flooded Alex's mind.

Suddenly something moved and Alex sensed another presence, though he couldn't see a face.

"Oh, yes," said Centauri. "Say hello to my assistant, Beta."

Alex reached out to shake hands and—*zap!* A small spark passed between their palms, making Alex recoil.

Alex strained, but he couldn't see any of Beta's features in the dark. And before he could look any closer, Beta hastily got out of the car.

"What about my prize?" said Alex.

"Ah, yes, I really must congratulate you," responded Centauri, "on your virtuoso performance. I've seen 'em come 'n' go, but you're the best, m'boy, dazzling, light-years ahead of the competition. Which is why Centauri's here—he's got a little proposition for you."

"What kind of proposition?" Alex was suddenly wary again.

"It involves the game."

Maybe the company wanted him to give demonstrations, Alex thought. Surely they had to pay him for that. "Sounds good, I guess."

"Bravo! I knew you'd say that." Centauri turned to his controls. "Now you must meet your fellows."

There was a *whoosh* as the gull-wing doors came slamming down and locked tight. The engine seemed to whine instead of rumble as Centauri peeled out of the parking lot like it was the final lap at Indy. Neither did he slow down upon entering the highway, ignoring the stop sign at the intersection. Instead, he accelerated, indifferent to the curves as they began to climb into the hills.

Alex, wide-eyed, was shoved back into his seat by the unexpected acceleration. Inside the car, all was silent.

"Where are we going? Where are you taking me?" Alex shouted.

"Handles well, doesn't she?"

The car continued to accelerate. Alex watched little white posts flick past his window, one right after another. They were highway mile markers. He knew they were traveling too fast now for him to think of doing anything, but if this madman ever slowed down . . . He reached over to check the door handle. There was no door handle. Now the mountain landscape outside was little more than a blur, dark shapes blending into one another.

"What are you doing?" he asked desperately.

"I want to keep it a surprise."

The car shuddered. Short, stubby fins emerged from the rear of the vehicle. As it exited a tunnel, the car left the road-bed, soared over wooden barriers and vaulted high over the edge of a sheer cliff which dropped away. It did not fall but continued to shoot skyward. Leaving our moon far behind, the Starcar streaked through the universe, heading for parts unknown.

Alex looked out the window and was surprised to see how small and vulnerable Earth looked. Again he was jerked back into his seat. The next time he was able to move about and look outside, the Earth had disappeared. No sign of the moon, either.

"That's enough," Alex said, wondering if he sounded half as hysterical as he felt. "Take me back—take me home!"

"Now don't be in such an all-fired hurry, son. All in good time. Sit back and enjoy the ride." Alex noticed his abductor was wiping at his face with a thin rag of metal mesh. When he turned to face Alex again, he was still smiling.

Only now his mouth was all wrong. In fact, his whole face was all wrong. His eyes were too big for the face, for any human face, but the face they were attached to wasn't in the least bit human. It was grotesque and distorted.

Alex's fists froze. He settled back in his seat to gape silently at the thing sitting in the pilot's chair.

Minutes passed. The creature used the metal rag on its face again. When it turned a second time, the familiar Centauri was smiling back at Alex.

Some kind of optical illusion, Alex tried to convince himself.

"Now," Centauri announced amiably, "it's time to go to supralight drive."

"Faster than light? That's impossible." Alex regretted the words the instant they left his mouth.

Alex felt the universe around him change. Stars danced in his eyes and he couldn't be certain if they were in front of or behind his corneas. But the colors were pretty. Space travel as psychedelia.

Alex's mind was lulled to sleep by the steady tick-tick of the control panel while the perfect environmental controls of the ship relaxed his body.

The ticking was interrupted by a sharp beep. Outside, the stars resumed their normal appearance. To the right, a pale green moon rich with copper ores was sliding past. A sun lay ahead. It was a little whiter than the one that baked the desert around the Starlite Starbrite trailer park.

Centauri, who had been sleeping, too, awoke and settled in to prepare for a landing as they dove straight for a cloud-shrouded planet, rich with ocher hues and not as blue as Earth.

"Hey, lemme out of here!" Alex pounded on his door. The door rose, and suddenly Alex wasn't so sure he wanted it open.

"Welcome to Rylos, my boy!"

"Rylos?" Alex remembered Rylos was the planet in the Starfighter game. "Rylos from the *game?*"

Centauri disappeared, and a female sergeant who was quite humanoid in shape gestured to Alex to disembark and follow her. She ushered Alex onto a people-mover, a moving sidewalk, which carried Alex past the Quartermaster, who handed Alex a uniform, boots, and helmet. He then went back to eating a space lizard on a hot-dog roll.

A massive ship was shunted past. Alex recognized it, and the other ships in the hangar. They were identical to those he'd manipulated so casually in the Starfighter video game.

"Gunstars. I gotta be dreaming. I gotta be."

A Rylan private inserted a small disk in Alex's ear. Alex blinked, reaching up to feel it while trying to balance the awkward bundle of clothing in his hand. The words of the Rylan sergeant came through to him clearly now, in unaccented English.

"You speak English?"

"I am not speaking your language," the Rylan informed him. "Your mind interprets my words via the translator button. It adapts to your own thoughts, transcribing the sense of what I say."

The sergeant started to usher Alex along. "Hurry, we don't have much time. The briefing begins immediately. Join the other recruits."

"Recruits?"

In the briefing area, twelve aliens, six wearing Starfighter uniforms and six wearing navigator's uniforms, turned to look at Alex.

A voice blared through a hidden speaker. "Attention, attention, attention! Ambassador Enduran of the Star League is here! He will deliver the final address."

The being who entered from the far side of the room and walked slowly toward the rostrum was Enduran, an aged and wise-looking diplomat. He ruled the Star League, an outer space United Nations.

He passed in front of an eclectic collection of creatures, all united in a common cause.

Trying to keep an eye on Enduran and his own path at the same time, Alex started working his way through the scattered seats.

"Excuse me . . . sorry . . . pardon me. . . ." He could only hope his apologies were being properly conveyed.

Inching his way to an empty seat, Alex's usual agility deserted him when he stumbled over a chair support, only to step back on something the size and shape of a garden hose. The hose whipped back like a retreating anaconda, throwing him off balance and toppling him into the lap of something with a face like a tormented cantaloupe.

The Tentacle Alien rose, blazing mad, eager for a fight. "Biped of a thousand pods! I should grind you to g'run dust!" A sweeping tentacle barely missed Alex's face.

"I'm real sorry, uh, sir." Alex let out a mental sigh of relief when the creature's anger seemed to subside. "It was an accident. I'm a stranger here. I just got in."

"No doubt it was an accident," said a friendly looking alien to his right. "Only a true fool would do such a thing deliberately. You don't trifle with a Bodati. They just love to fight. That's why they're perfect for this war."

"Excuse me, but you did just say 'this war'?"

The alien eyed him uncertainly, its gaze traveling from Alex's face down to the uniform he still carried.

"Why else do you think you're here? You have been recruited by the Star League to . . ."

That was more than enough to trigger Alex's memory. The rest he knew by heart. ". . . DEFEND THE FRONTIER AGAINST XUR AND THE KO-DAN ARMADA."

He'd been recruited because of his success at the game, he could be sure of that much now. By passing some carefully

constructed test disguised as a video game, he'd won the right to be carted halfway across the galaxy to participate in some upcoming war. No way, José!

Alex looked anxiously toward the exit, but all the doors had been sealed. He was stuck in the briefing room, at least until the Bodati moved. He might as well settle back and pay attention to the speaker.

There was sadness in the ambassador's voice, but also determination as he told the Rylans that the Frontier, a barrier of energy encircling the peaceful galaxy of the universe, was about to be destroyed because of a dark betrayal.

"The Frontier may be endangered from within our own ranks. We here on Rylos are especially vulnerable, since the traitor comes from this world."

He pointed over their heads, toward the line of sleek, powerful ships arrayed in the big hangar outside the briefing chamber.

"I am assured that our Gunstars, completely rebuilt and updated as they are now, acting under the command of the best Starfighters the League can muster, are more than a match for anything the Ko-Dan have built."

Enduran then explained that Rylans had evolved so far, had become so civilized, that they were not physically or mentally equipped to be Starfighters. "Peace breeds contentment and stifles the fighting reflexes and urges and what we might call the gift of doing battle.

"Among the millions of citizens of the League, only a few are left who still possess this gift." He let that sink in before adding, "The future of our civilization, of the League itself, rests on you—you, the most extreme throwbacks, the most primitive and yet skilled among us."

A cheer rose from the assembled fighters. Many of them were outcasts, social misfits. After this war, they would be regarded as saviors; not liked, perhaps, but respected. All looked forward to the forthcoming conflict.

All, that is, save one, who kept his thoughts to himself and wished desperately he were elsewhere.

Alex started shoving his way through the crowd, ignoring outcries of "Victory or death." In a few moments, he found himself nearly in the clear, on the opposite side of the chamber, where a familiar figure was vanishing around a far corner.

"Centauri! Centauri, wait!" Alex ran, waving and yelling, not looking where he was going and bumped smack into an alien, quite humanoid, though completely hairless. The creature had a rounded skull, and its face with its deep-set yellowish eyes was covered by a thick, brownish crust that reminded Alex of desert pondbeds, dried and cracked. The creature was carrying an armload of tools.

"I'm sorry," Alex apologized.

"This is a restricted area, off limits to—" The alien stopped in mid-sentence, examining the pile of clothes in Alex's hands.

"Excuse me, Starfighter. I am navigator/systems operator Grig. At your service, sir."

He performed an awkward salute, which Alex found interesting to see but impossible to duplicate, so he took the thick hand and shook it instead. Grig inspected his free hand thoroughly.

Alex nodded toward the line of waiting Gunstars. "You fly those?"

"Me, fly? You mean as an attack pilot? Dear me, no. I am a navigator and systems operator. I run the ship during combat, thus freeing Starfighters to do what they do best: attack and fight."

"Your job sounds tougher than the others."

"Not in the least. I merely have mechanical difficulties to cope with instead of mental ones. You are named?"

"I'm Alex Rogan. You called me a Starfighter. I'm no Starfighter, just a kid."

"Starfighter ability is not a function of age, Alex Rogan."

"Just Alex."

"Alex, then. It is a matter of a special combination of unusual talents: courage, flexibility under stress, the ability to make rapid decisions while under great pressure, reflexology, mental acuity, determination, and more. . . . You have been brought here to be a Starfighter, and you have been issued the uniform."

Alex shook his head violently. "Uh-uh. Not a chance I'm putting this on. I don't belong here. I told you, it's all been a big mistake."

Now Grig appeared uncertain. "Am I to understand that you are actually declining the honor of becoming a Starfighter?"

"You got it," Alex said with a relieved sigh.

"Extraordinary. For eons, all creatures have dreamed of becoming Starfighters. And you are actually turning it down. Tell me, where are you from?"

"Earth."

"Earth, earth," Grig mumbled. "Earth is not a formal member of the League. This is highly irregular. Who actually brought you here?"

"Centauri. And there he goes now." Alex waved him down. "Hey, Centauri!"

Alex was a little more than surprised when Centauri waved back and strode boldly to meet them.

"It seems we have a bit of a problem here, Centauri," Grig said quietly. "Did it ever occur to you that it's against the law to recruit from worlds outside the League? This may come as a shock to you, Centauri, but Alex doesn't choose to be a Starfighter."

It was a line of thought Centauri was not prepared for. His shock was clear.

"Doesn't 'choose' to be . . . but he has the gift!"

"Maybe he has the gift, but he doesn't have the inclination."

Centauri turned to Alex. "What's wrong with you, son? Are you a coward? Are you crazy? Don't you have any idea of the seriousness of the situation we face and of the singular tribute that's being paid to you?"

"I thought you were going to give me a prize. You never said a thing about my being singled out to fight in some nutsy interstellar war."

Their conversation was interrupted by a disturbance in the hangar. In minutes, everyone was aware of its presence among them. The light began to change, darkening at first near the center of the largest open area, then brightening as a flat white glow built into a solid globe of illumination. The light intensified, solidifying.

Alex whispered to Grig, "What is it?"

"Image projection. Somehow the Ko-Dan have learned the location of our command center."

Alex thought a moment. "The traitors Enduran mentioned. It has to be."

"Yes, the traitors."

"Are there many of them?"

"No, but there are enough to make a difference. They are not to be underestimated, nor is their leader."

"Xur." Alex stared fascinated at the rotating sphere of dense light and remembered details of the video game.

"Yes, Xur, but that is little more than a name to you. To us it conjures the image of a real person, of a great evil. Enduran knows this more than any other."

"Enduran? Why him?"

"Watch, listen, learn." Alex held his questions and did as he was told.

Within the spinning globe of light, a face began to take form. It resembled another he had recently observed, and Alex struggled to place it.

Enduran had appeared on the floor of the hangar. He approached the projection fearlessly. His expression hinted at anger barely held in check.

The projection reacted to this new presence, smiled humorlessly. "Hello, Father."

"Do not call me Father," said Enduran. "You are no longer my son. You are an outcast. You have returned for the good of Xur and Xur alone, with an armada of Ko-Dan warships behind you. Leave us in peace. Go back to exile."

Alex leaned close to whisper in Grig's ear. "Exile? Hey, Grig, what'd he do?"

"He tried to seize control of the Star League and have himself declared dictator. He's a scoundrel."

Xur and Enduran faced one another. "The Ko-Dan wish to be our friends," said Xur.

"The Ko-Dan are the reason our ancestors built the Frontier! And you wish to be a petty tyrant. Rylans will not let a dangerous and unbalanced child like yourself decide their future for them."

"And yet it was this 'child' who caught your master spy." Xur smiled darkly. "Hear me, Rylans!" Xur was all dictator now, addressing the assembly. "When the green moon of Galan is eclipsed, the Ko-Dan Armada under my command will invade. All who rise and join my cause will be spared. All who resist will wish for a quick death."

With that, the projection dissipated, and Xur's laughter faded to oblivion along with his contorted face.

Amid the rush of preparation for battle, Centauri turned to face Alex, his expression one of disbelief, and said, "You still wanna go, and miss all the excitement?"

Alex let the uniform fall to the floor of the hangar. "Get me outta here!"

"Okay!" Centauri muttered. "Home to Mommy. I give up."

Out in space, the Ko-Dan command ship, an immense and evil craft, burned into the Frontier with torch beams.

Inside the ship, a trembling Underling, Xur's personal servant, walked along a corridor, carrying a black scepter.

A shiny globe tipped the long staff he carried. The black metal orb concealed an impressive array of ultraminiaturized electronic components beneath its smooth black finish.

The Underling was brusquely stopped at the door to the command center by two Ko-Dan drones.

"Emperor Xur ordered me to bring his scepter."

"What transpires?" inquired the noble Kril, the Ko-Dan commander, from his position inside the center.

"An Underling, Commander," said one of the guards. "He carries a weapon."

"Scepter of Office," the Underling protested, keeping his voice deferential.

Xur, tall and imperious of manner, moved next to Kril and waved casually toward the doorway. "Yes, I sent for my scepter. Let him enter."

The senior guard did not respond to Xur's command but looked at his Ko-Dan master, Kril, for the order. Kril nodded. The Underling advanced, holding the scepter out before him.

Kril, angered by Xur's bombast, said, "It takes more than a scepter to rule."

"You are right, Kril. It does take more than a scepter."

Xur touched a concealed switch and a blade, glistening and deadly, emerged from the scepter's black globe. Xur waved it around the room with disconcerting casualness, but Kril never flinched.

The voice of an outraged senior officer became barely audi-

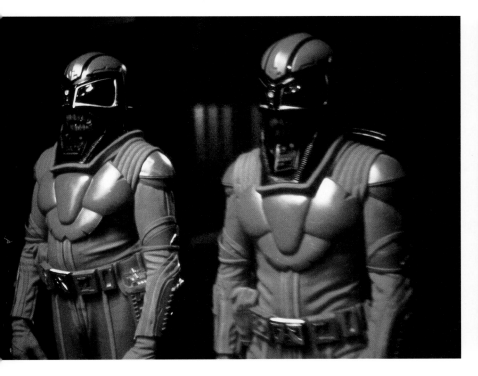

ble. "How long must we be forced to endure this fool . . . !"

"We have a break in the Frontier," a Ko-Dan private announced. Immediately the confrontation between the two leaders was forgotten amid the general excitement.

"Then the time has come." Kril's eyes glistened with anticipation. "Fire the meteor guns."

Hearing this, Xur slammed the nearest console with his fist, enraged. Ko-Dan they might be, but in this time and place *he* was master.

"Only I will give the order to fire! Is that understood?" Xur looked squarely at Kril as he spoke, then turned grandly to the proper station. "Meteor gunners. Fire."

The meteors came through a newly opened hatch, roaring through space from the hole in the Frontier. Guns continued to fire more and more meteors until a meteor shower appeared to be thundering through the breach.

Sitting at his console, a Rylan technician suddenly saw a bleep appear on his screen. "I show unidentified incoming objects, sir," he said to his commanding officer.

The sergeant stood over the technician as the console started to buzz. The blips loomed larger and larger.

The sergeant grabbed a mike and hit an alert button. "We are under attack. I repeat. We are under attack."

Scrambling Rylans rushed to their battle stations. Starfighters ran for their helmets and started climbing into their Gunstars.

No one noticed the Rylan Bursar making his way along the service conduit that ran behind the main war board. He did not belong there. The traitor placed a small pulsating device, an explosive charge, on the console, and retreated quickly.

Considering the small size of the package, the resultant det-

onation was substantial. It effectively demolished the war room, along with all local communications, thereby knocking out the Rylan defenses. A second similar package exploded simultaneously in a heavily guarded power station buried in the mountain range. In no time, the Rylan base was oblitered in a series of deadly meteoric explosions.

Mixed in with the rubble were the Gunstars, the Starfighters and the hopes of the Star League.

On the command ship, where there was a feeling of elation at the victory, Xur strutted about as if he had done it all.

"At last it is done!" shouted Xur. "Soon the Frontier will be down. They will all bow to their new emperor."

While Xur raved in the middle of the command center, the Ko-Dan smiled to themselves and quietly worked at their stations. One communications officer was concentrating on a single, tight-beam coded channel that emanated from the surface of Rylos. It was the fleet's only means of communicating with their Xurian allies below.

"Commander, the Xurian spy reports that one ship has escaped. It could be piloted by a Starfighter."

Xur whirled from the screen and the world it revealed. "A Starfighter escaped?"

Kril sighed, held his temper. "It is only one small ship. What can one ship do against the armada?"

"Track it," Xur snapped. "If it goes to supralight, take an energy reading and approximate place of reemergence into real space."

It was dark at the crossroad. The Starcar had reentered the Earth's atmosphere over the southwestern United States after midnight. It had set down safely on an unused dirt road, rumbled out onto the highway heading toward the trailer park and promptly broken down.

Centauri crawled under the hood to fix the car, his spindly legs and gartered socks jutting from under the vehicle.

"Sure I can't give you a hand?" asked Alex.

The old man spoke from beneath the car. "Ever done any work on a missealed sisendian toroid?"

"Uh, is that anything like a transmission?"

"Not really."

"Then I'm afraid I wouldn't be of much help." Alex turned to gaze down the highway. "It's only a couple of miles from here. I'll walk it. So long, Centauri. Nice knowing you."

"Wait a minute, boy, wait!" The old man struggled out from beneath the vehicle, wiped sand from his false face and fumbled in a pocket until he produced what appeared to be a slimline digital watch.

"Here." He held out the watch.

Alex shook his head. "Gee, I can't take a present from you."

Centauri shook his head. "This little toy functions as a watch, but that's only concealment. It's a short-range narrow-line communicator. If you prefer, think of it as your second chance, my boy. Should you change your mind regarding the employment I so diligently secured for you, just tap the communocrystals."

"Keep it. I won't be needing it."

"Just think it over, my boy," Centauri pleaded. "If nothing else, it's a perfectly serviceable watch."

Alex was tired of resisting Centauri. "All right. I'll hold on to it, if you insist. But I'm not changing my mind."

Centauri moved to the gaping gull wing on the driver's side of the car and put one foot inside. "You're walking away from history. History!"

Watching him depart, thinking about what Centauri had just said, Alex strapped the communocrystals to his wrist and started back toward the trailer park.

Arriving at his trailer, he opened the door quietly and tip-toed through the living room, past the tiny kitchen and into his bedroom. As he picked his way through the clutter strewn around the room, his gaze rose to his brother Louis asleep in the top half of the bunk bed.

Alex sat quietly on the edge of the lower bunk and started to untie his sneakers when suddenly he saw a shape moving beneath the covers. He leaped off the bed and whirled to stare at the shifting sheets and blankets, his eyes widened.

"Who's there?"

"Hey, keep it down," the voice under the covers said. "You're gonna wake Louis!"

A figure sat bolt upright in his bed. It was a mirror image of himself.

"Hey, you look like me!"

"Shush. Of course I look like you. I'm the Beta Unit."

"What on earth's a Beta Unit? I know what a Betamax is, but not a Beta Unit."

"A simuloid. An exact duplicate of you. Only not as loud. We met before," the alien continued. "It was in Centauri's car. Remember now? In the back. We touched hands, I took a fast impulse and retina scan, and then I got out fast. After which I became you."

Alex struggled to retain his composure. "Glory be! I've been replaced by a robot."

A truck ground to a halt outside the general store and a scruffy-looking hitchhiker jumped out. The hitchhiker watched as the lights of the truck were swallowed in the distance; then he headed into the trailer park.

BLEEP! BLIP! BLAM!

Electronic whizzes and buzzes lit up the video game as the hitchhiker walked past. At such close range the video explosions caused the hitchhiker's image to jam, revealing him to be an alien.

In his room, Alex rose from his chair and headed toward the door. "You're going back with Centauri right now!" he informed his double.

Just then Alex noticed that Louis had awakened and was sitting up on the upper bunk.

"Back to sleep, Louis, or I'll tell Mom," Alex said, facing the upper bunk.

From below the bunk, Louis's brother added, "You're blowing it, Alex. You're ruining everything."

Just conscious enough to be confused, Louis swung his head over the edge of the bunk. Seated below, to his great surprise, was his brother. So then who had just shouted at him from near the door?

"I said," the Beta Unit told the hanging face, "back to sleep, Louis, or I'll tell Mom!"

The ten-year-old threw the covers over his head.

Alex, confident that Louis would be staying under those

covers for a while, headed outside, tapping the crystalline face of his new "watch."

As Alex neared the edge of the awning of a nearby trailer, something cold and irresistible seized him from above and wrapped itself tight around his neck. Alex managed to turn in to the powerful grasp just far enough to find himself staring into the bulging face of the Alien Hitbeast.

As the alien raised a pistol, Alex wrenched with all his strength and managed to slide free of the alien's single-handed grip. He then ran blindly, dodging the alien's shots and tapping frantically on his communocrystals. "Please, Centauri, come in! Centauri, help! Something's trying to kill me!"

Alex stumbled, breaking the communocrystals to pieces. Dust fell on his face as he looked up to see the Hitbeast, standing on the edge of a roof, beading his interstellar pistol for the kill.

Standing nearby and thumbing his nose at the killer was the Beta Unit, who had followed Alex. The confused alien hesitated, but only for a moment, before taking aim again at the real Alex. But a violent *buzz-blast* hit the alien from one side, and he whirled. *Buzz-blast. Buzz-blast.* A fusillade zeroed in on the Hitbeast, cutting off one arm.

Centauri's Starcar fishtailed in front of the porch. The old man was firing through a port in the gull-wing door, his weapon shooting a deadly salvo up at the Hitbeast.

The alien keeled over. Smoke and steam poured from its body. It twitched once before tumbling off the roof and landing with a dull thunk on the gravel below.

Centauri slipped his weapon back into an outlandish shoulder holster. "Get a good look at that creature, Alex," Centauri said. "That is a Zando-Zan. A recruited murderer. He was sent to find and kill you, compliments of Xur."

"Xur! Why is he trying to kill me?"

Behind them, smoke still rose from the alien torso. One eye opened partway and searched the ground. Nearby lay the deadly pistol.

The alien gazed at its disembodied hand, willing it to move. Slowly the creature's fingers moved, lifting the blaster, inching it into firing position and aiming at Alex, who was deep in conversation and thought the alien was dead. *Buzz-blast.*

Crying out to warn him and leaping into the path of the incoming round, Centauri shielded Alex and fired back, zapping the alien creature with his own hidden weapon. The alien's body burst into sputtering flames and disintegrated.

But Centauri was shot himself. He staggered a beat and fell. Alex and Beta jumped to his side to help him.

"I'm okay, boys. It's just a scratch." Centauri gasped as he stood up and walked around to the driver's side of the Starcar, then turned to confront Alex. "Face it, Alex. You're a born Starfighter."

Exhausted and shocked by his brush with death, Alex knew that it was only a matter of time before another killer was sent to get him.

"All right, Centauri. Let's go."

Alex was anxious as they reached Rylos and descended to the portion of the northern continent where the supposedly secret Starfighter base was located. At least, the secret base *had* been located there, Alex corrected himself. The mountain in which it had been buried looked like a volcano that had blown itself apart. Whole forests lay flattened like toothpicks on the surviving slopes, and the topography had been rendered unrecognizable.

"Centauri. The base . . ."

Centauri came in from behind the sun to avoid detection by any lurking Ko-Dan ships. The entrance he located was partially blocked by debris but still passable. He slipped inside, narrowly missing several immense chunks of granite that had fallen from above. He coughed hard and squinted at the controls.

Alex leaned forward, concerned. "Are you sure you're all right?"

"I'm fine, just fine, my boy." He coughed again, then quickly wiped the blood from his lip so Alex wouldn't spot it.

The Starcar made a rough landing, coming to a halt in a damaged docking bay in the midst of wounded Rylans being attended by medics.

"Centauri." Alex reached for the alien and his hands came away covered with blood.

"Hey, somebody, help! Somebody get a doctor, we need a doctor here!" Alex ran around to Centauri's side of the car to pull him out when a familiar figure appeared, running toward him.

"Grig!"

The alien slowed, his near-rigid lips straining to convey his surprise. "Alex? You came back!"

Grig helped Alex pull Centauri's limp body clear of the car. Rylan medics appeared immediately and bent to tend to the injured Centauri, but to no avail. He was no longer alive. Grig stooped and closed Centauri's eyes.

"He saved my life," Alex muttered disconsolately.

Grig spoke sternly. "We've no time for mourning, Alex. The Frontier could collapse at any moment. Come along, come along."

"What happened here?" asked Alex as they walked through the destruction.

"The Ko-Dan attacked. Simultaneously, our defenses were sabotaged by Xur's fanatics. We were helpless. You've come back none too soon."

Grig stopped for a moment and, looking at Alex imploringly, said, "Are you ready to participate in the fight?"

"Well, yeah. Okay, sure."

"Interstellar, my boy, interstellar."

"But with what?"

"Come."

He followed Grig out of the devastated storage area and into a still-functioning elevator.

No point in wasting time, he thought as he climbed out of his jeans and shirt and into his Starfighter uniform.

The doors opened onto a well-lit chamber. A single ship sat gleaming in its docking bay.

Alex stared at the sleek ship, then scanned their surroundings as Grig led him downward. "Where are we?"

"In the design silo, on the far side of the mountain."

"Is this my Gunstar?" asked Alex.

"Yes," said Grig.

Grig stepped past him at the hatch door and eased himself into his navigator's chair. "Here's where I'll navigate, monitor life support and propulsion systems."

"And where do I sit?"

"In the gunnery chair, way up there."

Bvrrrrrrrrr—Grig switched on a small lift that elevated Alex to the gunnery chair.

Alex climbed into the chair, bumping his head on the display module as the chair suddenly swiveled.

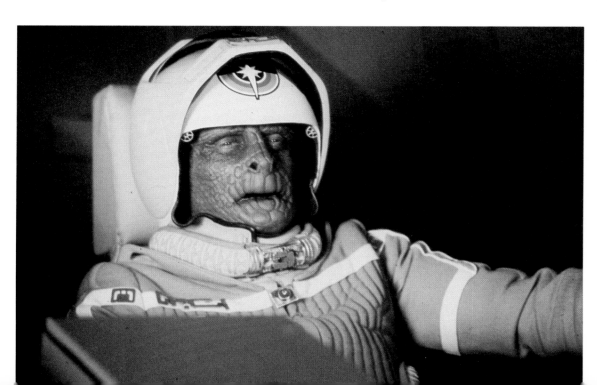

"Ouch! Whoa!" He leaned back from the display module, settling deeper into his seat. "Now what?"

"Put your left arm into the left arm lock and grasp the combat flight controller."

Alex did as he was instructed. A small control panel slid into position beneath his right hand.

"At your fingers now are the ship's weapons systems."

Alex moved slightly to inspect the panel and was startled to see that he recognized it.

"Hey, fan lasers, photon bolts, particle beams—just like on the game back home, except for this . . ." Alex moved his thumb toward a large red button.

"Careful, careful!" Grig shouted. "That's the Death Blossom. A weapon of last resort. Hopefully we won't have to use it."

"I'll go along with that." Alex studied the button warily. It looked like a big fat spider now, hunkered down on its legs, just waiting for a chance to jump out and bite him on the back of his hand.

"How come you know so much about this ship when it wasn't even included with the others?"

"I was working here with the design staff when the main hangar went up."

"Huh? When did the hangar go up?"

"When Xur attacked."

Alex paused. "What about the other hangars, the other bases?"

"What other bases?" Grig asked him.

Alex's thoughts were moving fast now, one right on the heels of the other. "You mean all the Gunstars were located in that one hangar?"

"Yes. We were overconfident and underexperienced."

"Well then, what about the rest of the Starfighters? The ones I sat with when Enduran spoke?"

"They were all in that one hangar." Grig's tone was flat and unemotional, wholly professional.

"You mean they're all dead?"

"Death is a primitive concept. I rather like to think of them as battling evil in another dimension."

Alex swallowed before asking the inevitable next question. "How many are left?"

"Counting yourself?" The ship shook beneath Alex's backside now, trembling with energy held in check, eager to show its strength.

"Yeah, counting myself."

"One." Grig touched a switch. A section of mountain vanished in front of them. Alex was slammed back into his seat as the Gunstar exploded skyward. The surface of Rylos receded behind them as the gimbal-mounted seats clicked into battle-ready positions.

Alex hoped he hadn't heard correctly. "Hold it, Grig. There's no fleet, no other Starfighters? One ship. You, me, and—that's it?"

"Precisely." Grig was unperturbed by Alex's tone.

"It'll be a slaughter," Alex said with a groan. "One ship against the whole armada!"

"Forget reality, Alex. Make a game of it if it helps. You might want to squeeze off a few rounds while you have the chance, work the bugs out of the system."

Grig manipulated some controls, and target lights shot from the ship's aft section and streaked across the Gunstar's bow.

"You're looking at false images projected by the drones," explained Grig. "They're designed to simulate the actual size of enemy vessels. Proceed on the assumption that you're firing at a real target. Remember—relax, stay steady. Take your time.''

"Okay.'' Alex took grim aim at the target lights. He sprayed them with fire, missed several, and nicked one. He fired again, the second time scoring many hits.

"Hey, that wasn't so hard.''

Now Grig projected a simulated image of the Ko-Dan Armada breaking through the frontier on the Heads-Up display screen. "The armada will break through here and reach Rylos in twenty clicks. Squadrons of deck fighters will precede the Mother Ship.'' Grig switched the image to the Mother Ship.

"Squadrons. How many squadrons?''

"Oh, it's not the number of squadrons that concerns me,'' said Grig as he magnified the command-ship image to the aft section, focusing on the communications turret, "but this control turret that sends out the commands to the deck fighters enabling them to act as one during a fight.''

"Then we gotta destroy the control turret,'' said Alex.

"And attack the fighters,'' added Grig, "while there's confusion in the ranks, before they rush Rylos. That's an excellent plan.''

Alex did some quick figuring. "Wait a second. We knock out the control center to prevent the fighters from acting in concert, but to get to the command center we gotta get through the fighters.'' He slumped. "We're dead.''

"Don't fret. I'll have it all figured out by the time we reach attack position.''

A steady humming noise suddenly penetrated the cockpit.

"What's that?" asked Alex.

"Sensor. We're nearing the Frontier."

Finally glimpsed, the infinite barrier loomed closer and closer. A buzz replaced the steady humming. Grig's main monitor screen came to life. Two images appeared off to port.

"Xurian ships," announced Grig. "I'll jam their transmissions so they can't report back to the rest of the armada, but we have to stop them quickly. Stand ready, Alex. There are your first live targets."

"Live?"

Ahead, the two Xurian ships suddenly disappeared, vanishing from their screens.

"Where'd they go?" Alex wondered.

"Only one place to hide from scanners at this range. Hang on."

The Gunstar dipped as Grig flung it toward a large asteroid drifting nearby. Alex flinched, but there was no rending crash. Grig had plunged them into the center of a large crater, close on the track of the fleeing Xurians. He slowed immediately, knowing their quarry would be forced to do likewise or risk smashing into the walls of the volcanic vent.

"Three clicks to kill zone. Weapons armed."

Alex leaned forward. "Grig, wait!"

"Fire when ready."

The images of the two Xurian ships were sharp on the screen floating in front of Alex's face, both of them pinned against the firing grid like tired butterflies. Alex stared blankly, suddenly conscious of what the pair of points represented.

"Fire, Alex, fire!"

"It's no good, Grig! I can't do it. Turn back, get us out of here, I can't!"

The tunnel ahead ballooned into a vast, open, airless dead-end cavern. The Xurians whirled around and sped back, straight toward their pursuer.

"Shoot, Alex!"

Blam! Blam! Blam! Blam! Alex's fingers danced on the fire controls. Energy shot from the Gunstar. The ship, shaken by the nearness of the destruction, trembled violently.

The Gunstar accelerated very slightly. Grig was turning toward another exit. The instant they reached the broken upper lip of the crater, the cockpit came alive with half a hundred warning lights.

Neither of them had to resort to instruments to see the Xurian ships resting on the surface of the planetoid. At the same time, their presence was detected by the five vessels they had surprised.

"A Xurian base!" Grig exclaimed. "This must be one of their rendezvous points with the Ko-Dan."

Blam! Blam! Blam! A fusillade of deadly Xurian fire bracketed the Gunstar from all sides.

Alex's fingers flew over the fanner gun controls, unleashing a burst of 360-degree fire. Some of the Xurian ships were pulverized instantly. Others exploded, completely destroyed.

It was all over quickly. Alex sat back in his seat as Grig moved them away from the asteroid.

"That was superbly done, Alex."

"Maybe," said Alex in response, "there is a Starfighter left."

The moon was close and full as it sat on the mirror of the lake's surface. The cars remained parked well back of the wooden sign that said Silver Lake.

Jack Blake's fancy pickup was one of the assembled cars. It stuck out from the battered Chevys and minipickups like a cabbage among brussels sprouts. From below the parking area, whispers and giggles were interspersed with the sound of the lake lapping against the yellow sand.

The police cruiser that pulled into the lot moved slowly, running on parking lights only. Inside, disguised as a policeman, a Zando-Zan designate, cousin to the first alien killer Centauri had blasted into oblivion, surveyed the silent ranks of vehicles.

Then he checked to make certain his radio was off and his gun was secure in its holster. He opened the door and stepped out. Eyeing pickup beds as well as interiors, he commenced a careful check of each vehicle.

Maggie and the Beta Unit had settled farther up the beach, away from everyone else, and the Beta Unit was having his problems. His hasty programming had included nothing about how to deal with his present situation, which was Maggie's desire for affection. Obviously a ticklish confrontation. One wrong move could wipe out his original's relationship with this female. As a professional, the Beta wanted desperately to do the right thing by Alex.

"Hey, Earth to Alex," Maggie was saying. "You're not even paying attention to me!"

There had to be a way out of the quandary in which he found himself. He glanced to his right. Jack didn't seem to be having any trouble making the proper social connections. He and his partner were whispering without pause, communicating fluidly. Beta listened to their conversation carefully.

"Darling, forgive me," Blake was apologizing to his girl.

Beta thought the apology reeked of insincerity, but nothing ventured, nothing gained, he decided. Turning back to Maggie, he pleaded, "Darling, forgive me."

"You're my Juliet, my Venus," Blake murmured.

Higher on the sand, the Beta whispered throatily, "You're my Juliet, my Venus."

Maggie sighed in Beta's arms, her eyes closed tight.

This approach seemed to be working. Maggie liked these Earth expressions. All Beta had to do was keep mimicking Blake.

"The other girls," Blake whispered, "they meant nothing to me."

"The other girls," Beta echoed, "they meant nothing to me." Beta then kissed Maggie and waited for her next reaction. There was a reaction all right, but not quite the one Beta had anticipated.

"What—other—girls?" Maggie inquired through clenched teeth, jerking away from him.

Was it something I said? the Beta wondered.

Meanwhile, from his position in the bushes overlooking the beach, the alien had focused on Maggie and Beta. He quietly removed the pistol from the holster at his hip. Just as he raised it, Beta spotted him and lunged toward Maggie.

"Get down."

Whoosh! Beta was struck by the silent alien shot as he tackled Maggie to the ground.

Maggie pushed against him, trying to get up. He didn't budge. Strong as she was, she couldn't move him an inch.

"Alex, have you been working out? Alex, let me up!" She hadn't realized what happened and was still very annoyed at him.

"I can't, and stop squirming. They're shooting at us."

Either it didn't register or else she didn't believe him.

"What are you talking about, Alex? I swear I don't understand you anymore."

Beta was out of patience pretending, and he sensed the situation was far too serious not to level with Maggie. "I'm not Alex. I'm a duplicate of him. I'm covering for him here while he saves the Star League from the Ko-Dan."

"You're elevator's not going all the way to the top, is it, Alex?" Maggie mumbled, gaping at him.

Exasperated beyond words, the Beta pulled open his shirt. Then he opened his chest. There was no blood, and after flinching in horror for a split second, Maggie found herself staring at a metal surface spotted with small ports and windows. Behind the transparencies, lights glowed steadily or winked on and off according to an intricate pattern.

"I'm a robot. Get it?"

"Gggg-gggg!"

The Beta spoke calmly as he refastened his artificial skin and clothing. "Just keep down. I don't want you killed by a shot meant for me."

There would be no second shot, however. The Zando-Zan had seen and heard enough. It rose and bolted for the stolen police car. The Beta saw him and took off in pursuit, cursing the sand that slowed him.

"Alex!" Maggie was struggling to follow. "Alex—or whatever you are—wait for me!"

Back inside the stolen police car, the Zando-Zan fumbled with the controls and finally activated the engine. The cruiser roared out of the parking lot.

Without hesitating, the Beta jumped into the nearest available vehicle, which happened to be Jack Blake's precious pickup. As he prepared to shift into drive, the door on the passenger side opened.

"Wait!" Maggie yelled.

"Let me go!" Beta yelled back. "If that assassin reports in to Xur and the Ko-Dan that I'm not Alex, then Alex is in big trouble. Stay here!"

"I'm not staying anywhere until I find out what's going on!" Maggie pulled herself up into the cab as the Beta peeled out.

Activity of a different kind reigned aboard the ships of the Ko-Dan Armada. Final preparations were underway. In the command room, a subofficer turned from his console. "We are ready to break through, Commander."

Xur entered the room and smiled. "Invade."

The Ko-Dan Armada moved ahead toward the frontier.

The police car ripped through brush with wild disregard for the large trees in its path. Finally it encountered one tree that refused to bend. The car banged to a halt in a rising ball of dust and dead leaves and was abandoned by its driver.

Running toward his spaceship, the Hitbeast dashed into a small clearing that was shaded from above by several much larger trees.

Once he was safely inside the ship, he began to compose a suitable message for his employers. He tapped out an interstellar version of Morse code.

Maggie clung to the overhead handle as the Beta sent the careening pickup hurtling across the rough desert road.

"You're a robot?"

"A robot."

"A duplicate of Alex . . . I can see that, of course. Then—where's Alex?"

The Beta jerked a thumb upward. "Out there."

"Alex—out in space. Is this for real?"

"Yes! Lethally real. Lethal to Alex if I can't stop that assassin before he tells his superiors what I've just told you."

On the command ship, an officer had just received and translated a message from Earth. "Commander Kril, we're getting a Zando-Zan signal on the alert frequency."

Xur interrupted. "I know what it concerns. Remember that single small ship that jumped to supralight just before we destroyed the base of Rylos?"

"Of course I remember." Kril was furious at being treated like some green subordinate.

"The message," continued the officer, "is from Zando-Zan Sixty-one. It says, 'The last Starfighter . . .'"

The Beta crashed through the brush and, reaching the edge of the small clearing, spotted the spacecraft's tower hatch and aerial. The Beta held the wheel firmly in one hand while opening its stomach with the other. It removed a small box no larger than a pack of cigarettes, stuck it beneath the pickup's dashboard and refastened his stomach.

"What's that?" Maggie asked, her teeth rattling.

"This will be a present for our friend. When I give the word, you jump."

"Only if this is going to help Alex—"

"*Jump!*"

Maggie jumped clear of the truck and landed on the ground. She looked up to see Jack Blake's pride-and-joy pickup truck with the Beta at the wheel smash into the spacecraft, stopping the message.

Both the pickup and the spaceship exploded, knocking Maggie off her feet.

"Well," Kril said into the unexpected silence, "what's the rest of the message?"

"I'm afraid that's all there is, Commander." The communications officer was apologetic. "That much came in, and then the transmission stopped."

Kril reflected, reading the part of the message that had gotten through. "'The last Starfighter . . .'"

"The last Starfighter," Xur declared portentiously, "is dead! Nothing can stop us now. Full sublight speed. On to Rylos!"

Alex shifted impatiently in his seat, itching for the fight to begin but aware that Grig would not take them out until just the right moment. Alex had watched as an armada of twenty to thirty small fighters had battered through the Frontier. But now something massive and dark appeared on his battle screen.

"The command ship."

"Yes, that's it," Grig said.

Alex smiled as Grig activated the Gunstar's oversize engines. Slowly they drifted out of the mouth of the crater under minimum power as the command ship lumbered majestically past.

"Weaponry activated," said Grig as the Gunstar suddenly erupted from the surface of the asteroid.

"Let's go!" Alex shouted, unable to contain the excitement he'd kept bottled inside him ever since they'd left Rylos. It was for real now. For real and forever.

The Gunstar exploded from the cave mouth, flying at incredible speed, and burned up toward the exposed underbelly of the command ship.

Alarms sprang to life within the command chamber of the flagship as the war consoles suddenly blared a warning, registering a hostile ship.

"What is it?" Kril turned instantly toward the detection station.

"Tracking," announced an officer.

Xur recognized it immediately. "A Gunstar—that's impossible!"

Kril turned angrily. "So: the last Starfighter is dead!" He glanced toward the head of bridge security. "This farce has gone on long enough. Seize him!"

A towering Ko-Dan officer advanced eagerly toward Xur, who snapped the blade from his scepter and aimed it at the alien, backing toward the doorway.

"How dare you? I'm the emperor of Rylos, by decree from your own emperor! I command you to . . ."

As Xur reached the heavy doors leading to the first corridor beyond, they parted, to reveal not a path of retreat but additional security personnel. They promptly grabbed him from behind and removed the deadly scepter from his grasp.

"Away with the 'emperor,'" said Kril. "All guns fire!"

Lights brighter than the distant stars suddenly filled the void around the Gunstar. Alex thought the display was beautiful, like a laser show at a rock concert.

"Three clicks to strike zone, Alex. Don't miss. We won't give another unopposed pass."

"Don't worry. I'm ready."

Then the command blister was in the center of Alex's floating battle screen. His fingers moved quickly, instinctively, over the fire controls.

"Now, Alex!" Grig shouted, afraid the moment would pass. Even as he spoke, the Gunstar's weapons systems fired simultaneously at the command ship as Alex fired photon bolts at the target. Flaming gas burst from the surface of the blister, enveloping it completely.

"Got it!" Alex yelled as he continued to pour fire into the flagship.

Xur and two Ko-Dan privates were walking along a corridor, passing a doorway, when suddenly the big flagship shook from the afterexplosions triggered by the devastating attack. The impact knocked them off balance, and Xur lunged, pulled his scepter from a drone and then killed the drone. Xur escaped through an airwell door. The last drone sounded the alarm at a small built-in wall communicator. "Alert! Xur has escaped!"

Xur's escape troubled Kril, but he had little time to deal with the flight of a single obstreperous Rylan. "Tell the extermination emissaries to seek and destroy him."

He steadied himself as still another explosion rocked the great ship. "Alert wing commanders."

The communications officer replied sorrowfully, "The fighter command center is gone, Commander. We have no way to direct our fighters."

"Look at them," Alex said excitedly as the Rylos-bound armada came within visual pickup range.

Alex started psyching himself up. "I've been recruited by the Star League to—"

"Life support good," said Grig. "Ammo packs at peak—propulsion at eighty—"

"—to defend the Frontier—and this is it—here we go."

The Gunstar dove upon four squadrons of Ko-Dan fighters that were advancing on two levels, vastly outnumbering it. Yet the Gunstar had the element of surprise. It fired on them, knocking many out with photon bolts and homing missiles.

It roared through the squadrons, pouring murderous fire into the ranks above and below it, vaporizing many of the craft in this initial onslaught.

An enemy commander looked up and down and, seeing this comet-flash of death coming for them, screamed orders as the Gunstar doubled back and wiped out three deck fighters.

Suddenly two sets of three fighters started to converge on the Gunstar from opposing sides, firing all they had.

Alex and Grig pounded the controls.

"We're hit! Watch the hull temp, Alex!"

"Evade!" yelled Alex.

Grig took the Gunstar into a steep vertical climb away from both sets of attackers. The charge ended in multiple destruction as the wildly aimed weapons of the opposing fighters blasted each other.

"Hull temp critical! The power packs are low! We need time to recharge!" Grig cried.

"Take us around Rylos," Alex answered.

As it raced around the planet, the Gunstar stayed just above the ionosphere, skimming the outer edge of the Rylan atmosphere and vanishing from the screens of those Ko-Dan ships alert enough to begin tracking it.

With the demand down on the ship's system, Grig was able to rechannel the drive, and the affected area returned to normal.

"Watch, Alex. We'll be back in attack range again in a minute or two."

They raced across the terminator, only to have their screens stay blank.

Alex hunted for telltale images, found nothing. "Hey, where's the armada? They must have run for it."

"That would not be like the Ko-Dan." Grig adjusted a control. Immediately both screens filled with ships at the outer limits of detection.

"Uh-oh. They did retreat, but only to reestablish communication with each other and with the flagship." Grig paused as several lights winked on. The multiple targets did not attack but began to encroach slowly on the Gunstar's position. "Englobement. A three-hundred-and-sixty-degree attack. The Circle of Doom."

Alex switched to a starward view, saw that the Ko-Dan had wholly encircled the Gunstar and the green moon.

"Get ready, Starfighter, because we're going to have to use the Death Blossom," Grig informed Alex.

"Remember, you have sixty seconds of full fire at close range—theoretically."

"Whaddya mean, theoretically?"

"Naturally, the Death Blossom has never been battle tested. It could overload the systems, blow up the ship . . ."

Alex hit a lever as Grig nodded, keeping a stiff upper lip. The Gunstar's hull unfurled into the deadly Death Blossom mode, spreading lethal tendrils in all directions.

As Alex watched the fighters advance, he wiped his palms, concentrating, ready.

"Wait till they're well within the Blossom's kill zone," cautioned Grig.

"Now?"

"Steady . . ."

"Now, Grig, now?"

"Fire!"

Alex hit all triggers, all weapons, in a flash of movement.

The Gunstar became a whirling dervish of firepower and destruction, and the battle zone resembled a swirling vortex of laser lights, death and debris. The wash swept Ko-Dan ships away as though they'd never been, vaporizing all before they had a chance to escape.

A warning buzzer sounded loud in the Gunstar. "Engines down, power down," Grig announced, studying his readouts. "Except for life support and communications, we're dead."

Exhausted, Alex pulled his arms out of the control sleeves and indulged in the ultimate luxury of wiping his face and rubbing his eyes.

"It doesn't matter, Grig. We did it."

Alex started to climb out of his chair as *bam! bam! bam!* Hostile fire streamed past the Gunstar. He and Grig looked up to see the command ship!

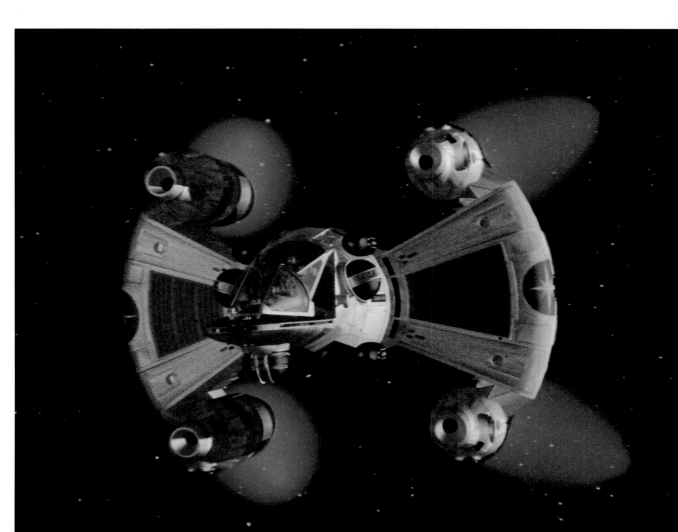

It was diving on them, firing all its guns, damaged but not dead by any means as it charged toward the Gunstar, which was close to the green moon of Galan.

Kril was at his command post as smoke filled the cabin. Watching the Gunstar loom larger and larger, he turned to a private.

"Why have you stopped firing?"

"Commander, our guns are out. Damage control is repairing them."

"Forget the guns!" shouted Kril. "Ramming speed!"

Alex stared at his screen. "Grig, they're moving toward us."

"I know, Alex."

"What are they doing?"

"I think they are actually going to try and hit us with their own vessel. What a remarkable notion."

"Remarkable, nothing. *Do* something!"

"I am trying, Alex. All we have left is a little stored power for communications and life-support maintenance."

"Switch it through to the drive and hold your breath!"

Grig tried to do so. The temperature in the cabin began to fall rapidly. No longer continuously recycled and freshened, the air started to become foul.

"Hurry, hurry!" Alex yelled.

The command ship loomed larger and larger. It was coming fast at them, ensuring certain death.

Finally Grig got power. The engines roared to life.

Alex hit the steering and the Gunstar pivoted, then dipped below the immense command ship. There was actual contact between the hulls, a rarity in space, unheard of in combat. The screeching sound produced by the scrape of metal against metal was deafening in the cockpit of the Gunstar.

Then as the huge command ship rumbled past, its delicate towerlike radar spire was shot away by Alex's final rounds. The command ship shuddered, plunged and exploded like a supernova.

With the Gunstar resting in the central square of the capital city of Rylos, Alex stood next to it. He was the decorated hero at this state occasion. Grig stood nearby, looking like a proud parent listening to the cacophony of cheering aliens shouting the Rylos equivalent of "Vive la Earthling!"

"Thank you, Ambassador Enduran," Alex was finally able to mutter, making the Rylan complimentary sign with his hands as Grig had taught him.

"Thank you, Starfighter," Enduran replied. He turned and gestured, whereupon the assembled officials, administrators and directors of the government of Rylos, in concert with the visiting representatives of the League, performed a half-bow toward Alex that left him feeling very strange indeed.

Suddenly Alex spotted an elderly figure standing amidst a group of aliens on a nearby mobile platform. Ignoring the crowd, Alex ran toward the newcomer.

"Centauri! You're supposed to be dead!"

The old man grinned. "I'm supposed to be a lot o' things, my boy, but deceased ain't one of 'em."

It was cold out. Or maybe it wasn't, but it felt that way to Maggie. She sat on the edge of the porch that ran across the front of the general store.

"Where are you, Alex? Too far away for me to imagine?"

"Alex?" another voice called out, a note of concern attached to it. That was Mrs. Rogan. How much should she be told?

Maggie recognized several of her friends along with Mrs. Rogan, and one nonfriend: Jack Blake.

"Maggie," Mrs. Rogan asked in a gentle but no-nonsense voice. "Where's Alex?"

"Where's my truck!" Blake yelled without giving her a chance to reply. "Where's your boyfriend?"

"Mrs. Rogan, it's like this about Alex. He isn't . . ."

Behind Maggie, the old weathervane atop the store began to spin wildly, even though there was hardly any wind. Dogs began to howl. They were joined by cats.

A crowd of alarmed residents ran out of their trailers and looked up to see a falling light. It was the underside of a spaceship that was lowering itself toward the parking lot. Maggie started walking rapidly toward it.

The spaceship touched ground, silent except for a deep internal humming.

"Far out!" yelled Louis. "We've been invaded!"

Something was descending from the belly of the spacecraft, a lift of some kind. A creature stepped off the lift and walked toward the crowd. Then it stopped in front of Maggie and removed its helmet.

"Alex!" Her face lit up as brightly as the ship's landing lights. "Alex, is it you?" She jumped into his arms, staggering him. "It is you! Alex, Alex, Alex. . . ."

"Maggie."

They kissed, and that was enough to bring the crowd of gasping onlookers shuffling close.

Mrs. Rogan pushed through the others. "Just where have you been, Alex?"

"Out," Alex said automatically, then added, "I've been on another planet, Mom. That's my Gunstar. . . ."

The lift was descending again. On it stood a tall alien shape. The crowd drew back fearfully.

"A monster!" one of the women shouted.

Maggie's granny was trying to push her way forward, clutching her old shotgun. Alex hastened to cut her off.

"Wait! Put down the shotgun, Granny. Everybody, come back. I want you all to meet Grig. My best friend."

He led Grig down an impromptu reception line. ". . . And this is my mom," Alex said as Mrs. Rogan eyed Grig warily.

Grig took Mrs. Rogan's hand. But instead of shaking it, he bent and put his lips to the dorsal side.

"You should be proud of your son, Mrs. Rogan," Grig said, remembering the little Earth language he had learned from Alex. He looked past her at the assembled crowd. "You should all be proud of him. He saved the League and hundreds of worlds, including Earth. He is the greatest Starfighter ever. And he will teach other potential Starfighters."

Then Grig cast a solemn glance at Alex. "Time to leave."

Maggie was stunned. "Leave?"

"Alex?" said Mrs. Rogan.

He kissed her gently on one cheek and nodded. "I have to, Mom. You heard Grig. I have a job to do. An important job. I promised."

"Gee, can I come too, Alex?" Louis asked, staring worshipfully up at his brother.

Alex kneeled until they were eye to eye. "Sorry, squirt. There's only room for me, Grig and Maggie."

She swallowed. "Me?"

Alex put his arm around her. "Of course. That's why I came back. You gotta come with me, Maggie. This is our chance. It's bigger than me, or even you and me. It's bigger than anything. I'm not just a kid from a trailer park up there. I'm a Starfighter."

"But Alex I can't go with you and leave everyone here behind. I'm scared."

From inside the ship, a voice sounded over a speaker, gentle but insistent. "Al-lex!"

"I can't talk anymore," he told Maggie. "Anyway, I've said everything. I gotta go." He hugged her hard, forcing himself to move on to his mother and Louis. Then he turned and headed for the waiting lift.

Haze filled the air as the ship's drive disturbed the atmosphere and irritated dust particles swirled above the parking lot.

Maggie kissed her granny good-bye, fighting back tears. Then she turned and ran for the ship, shouting and waving frantically. "Alex, wait, Alex!"

The lift was nearly into the belly of the Gunstar, but nearly isn't all the way. It stopped and lowered to the ground. Alex helped Maggie onto the platform and kissed her with great tenderness.

The Gunstar lifted quietly, the humming of its drive a muted thrum. Through its transparent canopy, Alex and Maggie could be seen. The Gunstar streaked upward, toward the indigo oceans of the universe, soon resembling a shooting star.